TERRANCE DICKS

THE
INCA ALIEN
INCIDENT

Piccadilly Press • London

First published in Great Britain in 2001
by Piccadilly Press Ltd.,
5 Castle Road, London NW1 8PR

Text copyright © Terrance Dicks, 2001
Illustration copyright © Andrew Skilleter, 2001

A catalogue record for this book is available from
the British Library

ISBN: 1 85340 663 5 (trade paperback)

1 3 5 7 9 10 8 6 4 2

Printed and bound in Great Britain by Bookmarque Ltd.

Cover design by Judith Robertson
Set in 12pt Palatino

Terrance Dicks lives in North London. He has written many books
for Piccadilly Press including the CHANGING UNIVERSE series and
the SECOND SIGHT series.

Also available in this series: *The Bermuda Triangle Incident, The Borley
Rectory Incident, The Circle of Death Incident, The Chinese Ghost
Incident, The Easter Island Incident, The Mafia Incident, The Nazi
Dagger Incident, The Pyramid Incident, The Transylvanian Incident*
and *The Wollagong Incident*

PROLOGUE

The temple was in ruins, overgrown by surrounding jungle.

Once it had been a place of incredible wealth and blazing glory, its walls covered with sheets of solid gold, studded with rubies and emeralds. Golden statues of men and women and animals, llamas and jaguars and sheep, once crowded its outer courtyard.

The gold was gone now, ripped away hundreds of years ago by greedy Spanish conquerors. But the basic outlines of the temple remained. At the top of a crumbling stone platform was the altar.

The altar of sacrifice.

Now, as the sun rose high over the Andes, the altar was once again in use.

Wearing only a loincloth, a man lay sprawled on his back, staring blankly up at the sky. A little group of robed worshippers surrounded him, crowding the terraced steps on each side of the pyramid. *Above him towered the High Priest, resplendent in feathered cloak and terrifying ceremonial mask. High above his head he held a huge sacrificial knife in a two-handed grip.*

As the first rays of the sun touched the altar the High Priest's eyes glowed red and the great knife swept down . . .

Chapter One

VIP TREATMENT

As the limousine turned into the Strand, I tugged irritably at the knot of my tie, which was doing its best to strangle me. I felt stiff and uncomfortable in dark trousers and a blazer, my nearest approach to a respectable outfit.

Dad looked at me benignly over his glasses.

'Something troubling you, Matthew?'

'I feel like a tailor's dummy,' I grumbled. 'What's it all *for*?'

'My dear Matthew, you know as much as I do. We're having lunch with Ms Alexander. There's somebody she wants us to meet.'

'Who?'

'She wouldn't say. Apparently it's to be a surprise.'

'So why all the dressing up? I mean, unless it's one of the Royal Family . . .'

Dad looked shocked. 'She's asked us to lunch at the Savoy, Matthew, one of London's finest hotels. A place that still maintains certain standards. If you turned up in your customary ruffianly outfit, they wouldn't let you in.'

By 'ruffianly outfit' he meant my usual jeans, trainers and T-shirt.

Dad himself was wearing his new grey suit for the occasion, just acquired at enormous expense from Saville Row. He actually *likes* dressing up.

'Besides,' Dad went on, 'anyone who rates the Savoy Grill is getting VIP treatment – which means whoever it is has to be important to her. And anyone who's important to Ms Alexander . . .'

He had a point there. Ms Alexander was a formidable figure. She was the head of a small top-secret intelligence agency, specialising in the offbeat and unusual. We'd worked with her several times before.

I'm Matt Stirling, by the way. The tall, bespectacled, beaky-nosed character sharing the limousine with me was my father, Professor James Stirling, all-round egghead and world famous space scientist. At least he used to be, until space research funds dried up. Somewhat unwillingly, he became Director of the Department of Paranormal Studies, set up by a big American science foundation.

At the same time he'd found himself landed with me. He'd split up with Mum when I was a baby and when she died in a car crash, I was brought up by relatives. When they retired to live abroad, Dad suddenly had a strapping teenager on his hands. He'd solved the problem by taking me out of school, taking over my education himself, and taking me on as his assistant.

Since then we'd lived and worked in sometimes uneasy coexistence. The trouble is Dad's used to being a VIP. He can be both arrogant and obstinate – and I'm pretty strong-minded myself.

Dad, of course, sees things the other way round.

The limousine turned into the short cul-de-sac that leads to the Savoy Hotel.

A commissionaire opened the door and we both got out. Dad automatically reached for his wallet but the driver shook his head.

'All taken care of, sir.'

Of course, it was an intelligence service limousine, I thought, sent by Ms Alexander to pick us up. The driver was probably James Bond in disguise. The car drove away and I wondered idly if it had built-in machine guns and an ejector seat.

We went into the lush foyer of the Savoy Hotel

and Dad strode into the Grill Room. It was much what you'd expect, all ornate decor, white table-cloths, gleaming silverware and soft-footed waiters wheeling trolleys bearing huge joints of roast meat.

Dad murmured Ms Alexander's name to a lordly *maître d'hôtel* and we were ushered to a secluded corner table.

I wasn't surprised by its position. Spies like to sit with their backs to the wall.

Ms Alexander rose to greet us as we reached the table. She hadn't changed. Small, neat, dark-haired and terrifyingly efficient, she was the sort of woman who ignores glass ceilings and sex discrimination and ends up running a multinational or the biggest merchant bank in the world.

'Thank you both for coming,' she said. 'Please, sit down. Let me get you an *aperitif.*'

A waiter appeared from nowhere and Dad ordered a kir, a mixture of white wine and cassis, alcoholic blackcurrant syrup of which he's particularly fond. I asked for a Coke. The waiter winced but bore up bravely.

The drinks arrived seconds later and Dad looked at the empty fourth place at the table.

'So, where's the mystery guest?'

'His plane was slightly delayed,' said Ms Alexander. 'He should be here any minute though.' She looked across to the Grill Room entrance. 'And here he is!'

We both turned and saw a small, slim, dark-haired man coming into the restaurant. As he approached our table we registered an immaculate dark suit, an olive complexion, a pencil moustache and brown eyes that gleamed with intelligence.

Dad looked baffled, but I recognised him at once. I jumped up as he reached our table.

'Carlos!' I corrected myself, 'I'm sorry! Colonel Santera, how do you do?'

'Please, amongst friends I prefer Carlos,' said Colonel Santera. 'I am very well, Matthew, and I trust that you are the same. And you, Professor!' He shook hands with us both, then leaned across the table, took Ms Alexander's hand and pressed it to his lips. 'And you, Maria, I trust I find you well?'

I won't swear Ms Alexander blushed, but her face softened for a moment.

'Very well, thank you, Carlos.'

A waiter appeared and Carlos ordered a champagne cocktail. When it arrived he raised his glass in a toast.

'To our happy reunion!'

We'd first met Colonel Santera some time ago on far-away Easter Island. We'd gone there to investigate some mysterious events involving the island's giant statues. He had introduced himself to us as Carlos, a humble native guide. It wasn't until later we'd realised that he was really Colonel Carlos Santera, the James Bond of Chilean Intelligence, sent there to help us.

Waiters appeared with menus and I was relieved to discover that the Savoy Grill wasn't too posh to serve an excellent steak and chips.

The meal was largely taken up with reminiscences of our adventures on Easter Island. It wasn't until the coffee stage that we got down to business.

'I have come to ask for your help, Professor,' said Carlos. 'Yours too, of course, Matthew.'

'I see,' said Dad, cautious as ever. 'In connection with what?'

'In connection with certain mysterious events in Peru,' said Carlos.

Dad frowned. 'Peru? I understood that you were in the service of Chile, Colonel Santera.'

'Chile and Peru are neighbours,' said Carlos. 'We have had our differences – the occasional war . . . these days we strive for better relations. Peru asked my government for help – specifically for *my* help.' He smiled modestly. 'I have a certain reputation. Perhaps the fact that I am myself half Peruvian had something to do with it. My mother's family came originally from Lima.' He spread his thin brown hands. 'At all events, they asked for me – and they also asked for you. In fact, they insisted!'

'Why us?' I asked.

Carlos shrugged. 'I imagine they know of our successful collaboration on Easter Island.'

'Perhaps I should add that this request has the full backing of the British Government,' said Ms Alexander. 'And, of course, of our American allies. Naturally, events in South America concern them very deeply.'

If Dad was impressed to learn that no less than three governments were after our services, he didn't show it. 'I see. And exactly what are we expected to do – about what?'

Colonel Santera paused, choosing his words.

'We want you to save Peru, perhaps all of South America, from exploding in bloody revolution.'

Not surprisingly, this turned out to be a bit of a conversation-stopper. There was a moment of silence. I decided someone had to get things moving. 'Sounds like a tall order,' I said. 'What's going on?'

Before Carlos could answer, Dad interrupted in his usual tactful fashion.

'Whatever it is, it's nothing to do with us. I want nothing to do with politics – especially South American politics!'

Carlos Santera's black eyes flashed angrily and Ms Alexander frowned. I decided it was time for a bit of diplomatic intervention – something I often have to do with Dad.

'Give the colonel a chance to explain,' I said. 'I don't suppose he's come here to ask us to put up election posters or do a bit of door-to-door canvassing in Lima.'

Dad had the grace to look embarrassed. 'I'm sorry, Colonel, that was rude of me,' he said stiffly. 'Please go on.'

Carlos grinned, as quick to forgive as to get angry. 'Your attitude is understandable, Professor. Personally, I prefer to stay out of South American politics myself! However, this particular problem has elements that bring it into your sphere of interest.' He paused again. 'You are familiar with South American history?'

'Reasonably so,' said Dad. He hates to admit he

doesn't know absolutely everything about everything.

'We once did a school project on the Incas,' I said. 'Taken over by the conquistadors in the sixteenth century, weren't they? Cortez and that lot?'

Carlos nodded. 'Cortez was in Mexico. In Peru it was Francisco Pizarro. He set off for Peru, lured by tales of a land rich in gold and jewels. He arrived in 1532 with less than two hundred men. In just a few years they conquered the mighty Inca empire.'

'Aided by the Western diseases they brought with them,' said Dad acidly. 'Diseases to which the native Indians had no resistance. Smallpox, bubonic plague, measles, whooping cough, influenza . . . Over the years, the native population shrunk to a sixth of its former size.'

I shuddered. 'You might call it an early form of germ warfare.'

'It is a horrible story,' said Carlos. 'Believe me, I feel for the sufferings of my Inca ancestors.' He caught my surprised look. 'Oh yes, there is Inca blood in my family, on my mother's side. However, that is all in the past.' He went on, 'For the next few hundred years Peru, like other South American states, was a colony of Spain, ruthlessly exploited for its gold and minerals, the Indians little better than slaves. Then, in 1821, Peru gained independence.' He sighed. 'For the Indians, nothing changed. The rulers got richer and the Indians, exploited as always, got even poorer.'

'South America has a fascinating history,' said Dad. 'Fascinating and terrible. But, forgive me, Colonel, I still don't see what it has to do with us. As you said yourself, what's done is done.'

Carlos smiled ruefully. 'Now, in the twenty-first century, some thought is being given to the rights of the Indians.'

'Too little and too late, as usual,' grunted Dad. 'The slash and burn policy has almost destroyed their native jungles, driven them to starve in shanty towns on the edge of your big cities. No wonder they're ripe for revolt.'

Carlos shrugged. 'I agree. There is still much to be done. But there is *some* improvement, a small gleam of hope. Now all that is at risk.'

'Why?' I asked.

'Because somebody wants to turn back the clock.'

I gave him a baffled look. 'How? Why? You don't mean the Spaniards are trying to take over again?'

Carlos smiled grimly. 'It is even more fantastic than that, Matthew. Somebody, some movement, some *force*, wants to restore the Empire of the Incas.'

'And how are they going to do that?' asked Dad scornfully.

'Simple,' said Carlos. 'Destroy or drive out the descendants of the conquering Spaniards, get rid of all the machinery of civilisation. Then, they say, everyone will live a happy and prosperous life under the rule of the Inca kings.'

'Ridiculous,' said Dad.

'Perhaps so,' said Carlos. 'But many of the Indians believe it. And they form half of the population of Peru. Then there are the *mestizos*, those of mixed Spanish and Indian blood – like myself. Many of them will support the Inca cause.'

'All the same,' said Dad, 'it's hard to believe that such an impractical plan has any chance of success.'

'Do not be so sure, Professor,' said Carlos. 'There are rumours of Indian revolt all over South America. Mexico, Paraguay, Colombia. If the Peruvian movement spreads . . .' He paused. 'There is something else. The one inspiring this movement is no ordinary revolutionary. He claims to be the reincarnation of Atahuallpa the murdered Inca king. Now it seems he has returned to exact a bloody vengeance. Already there have been sacrifices – human sacrifices.'

Chapter Two

THE MASK OF POWER

We listened as Carlos went on with his story.

It had started small, he said, a revival of interest in the old ways, the old ceremonies. But the idea had spread with astonishing speed. Wandering prophets and agitators had appeared, foretelling the restoration of the Incas to their former greatness. There were stories of a sacred mask that gave its wearer incredible powers; assassins with no fear of death because they believed they were immune to police bullets; ghostly apparitions of Inca priests at sacred sites; secret meetings and ancient ceremonies in remote jungle villages and in the shanty towns of the big cities. Then the sacrifices had begun. Bodies found in the ruins of ancient temples, their hearts ripped out in a ritual sacrifice.

'The first one caused a tremendous scandal,' said Carlos. 'A party of early-bird tourists visited the Sacred Stone in Machu Picchu, hoping to avoid the crowds.' He smiled grimly. 'They got more authentic Inca atmosphere than they'd bargained for. The Stone was running with blood and there was a body at its base. A body without a heart. After that there were more sacrifices, many of them. All over Peru people are being kidnapped from their homes and offices. Kidnapped and killed.'

'What sort of people are being sacrificed?' I asked.

'Authority figures,' said Carlos. 'Army officers, senior policemen, Government officials.'

'Any other links?'

'The victims are all men of pure Spanish blood.'

Dad nodded. 'It was always the Inca custom to sacrifice their prisoners,' he said. 'And if these people think they're fighting some kind of war . . .'

'It's a war they can't win,' said Carlos. 'It can only end in armed uprising. An uprising that will be savagely repressed – by Government troops with rifles and machine guns and helicopters. The Indians will be massacred.'

'The conquistadors all over again,' I said.

'Exactly,' said Carlos grimly. 'Only this time they will finish the job. The remnants of the Inca will be wiped out. Not only that, chances are the military will seize power again.' He looked appealingly at Dad. 'We mustn't let it happen, Professor.'

Dad was silent for a moment. 'It would be a terrible tragedy,' he said at last. 'But it's still a political problem, after all. I really don't see how we can help.'

'You can help Carlos to find this so-called reincarnated Inca king,' said Ms Alexander. 'He's obviously exploiting native superstitions. If you can expose him as a fake . . .'

'Suppose he isn't a fake?' I said. 'According to Carlos, this movement is spreading with unnatural speed. Things are happening that are hard to explain – ghosts, bullet-proof assassins. Suppose some kind of genuine paranormal power is involved?'

'Then you and your father can find some way to deal with it,' said Ms Alexander firmly. 'You've done it before.'

'Thanks for the vote of confidence,' I said wryly. 'All the same, I'm afraid Dad's right. It's really a political problem.'

'No!' said Carlos definitely. 'More than politics is involved. This movement is rumoured to have the support of the shamans, or some of them anyway. A shaman is –'

'I know what the word means,' snapped Dad. 'A kind of spiritual leader.'

'More than that,' said Carlos. 'A shaman is – well, it's a difficult word to define. Wise man, healer, prophet, sorcerer, magician . . . There are shamans all over South America. They're regarded with great respect and some of them are said to have extraordinary powers.'

'Would they support a movement like this?' asked Dad.

Carlos shrugged. 'Who knows? Some might.'

'It's still not much to go on.'

Ms Alexander said, 'Colonel Santera is convinced that paranormal forces are involved, and I think he's right. We need your help.'

Dad still looked doubtful. He turned to me. 'Matthew?'

I was surprised and pleased. For the first time he was treating me as a full partner. I thought for a moment. 'I think we have to try. Suppose Carlos is right and things work out the way he said? The ordinary Indians, the descendants of the Inca, have had a hard enough time already. If we can do anything to stop them being wiped out . . . and the world certainly doesn't need any more military dictatorships.'

'Very well,' said Dad. 'When do we leave?'

'Tomorrow,' said Ms Alexander. 'Your flights are already booked.' She caught Dad's eye and said hastily, 'Provisionally, of course. I'll confirm them at once.'

I looked at her innocent expression and repressed a smile. I was pretty sure there was nothing provisional about those bookings. She had known perfectly well that, after the usual protesting and grumbling, Dad would agree to go. He always did.

Dad looked at his watch. 'If we're leaving tomorrow, we'd better get moving. We've our packing to do.'

'Are you travelling with us, Carlos?' I asked.

Carlos shook his head. 'I leave tonight, by military jet. My journey will be quicker than yours, though less comfortable. I will meet you when you arrive.'

Ms Alexander ordered the bill. 'If you'll come back to the agency with me, we'll sort out the passports and travel documents. You'll go as guests of the Peruvian Government and so have diplomatic status.'

The bill arrived, Ms Alexander signed it and we made for the foyer.

As we came out of the Grill Room, a little group of dark-suited men came into the foyer. They all looked vaguely alike – olive complexions, dark hair and brown eyes, and they all had black moustaches. In the lead was a very tall, brown-skinned man with white hair and a neat white beard.

Carlos came to a sudden halt. 'Don Ramon!'

The tall man saw Carlos at the same time and raised a hand in greeting.

'Don Ramon de Escobar is attached to the Chilean Foreign Service,' said Carlos. 'He is also an associate of the Institute of Inca Studies in Lima. He is here on some kind of diplomatic mission.' Carlos smiled. 'He is a great scholar, and a great man. He is also my cousin. Forgive me, but I must pay my respects.'

We said hurried goodbyes, and Carlos promised to meet us in Lima. As we left the hotel we saw him hurry over to the tall man and bow respectfully.

The tall man smiled warmly and wrapped Carlos in a hug.

Dad sniffed. 'Emotional types, these Latin Americans!'

'Knock it off,' I said. 'You'll cause a diplomatic incident!'

Outside the hotel, Ms Alexander's limousine

appeared as if by magic and soon we were gliding away.

An hour or so later, after a brief visit to the Thames-side HQ of Ms Alexander's intelligence agency, we were in a taxi on our way back to Hampstead.

'We'd better stop at the deli on the Green and pick up some fresh pasta,' I said. 'We've nothing at home and we've got to pack tonight so we won't want to eat out.'

I'm no great cook, but even I can boil spaghetti and pour the sauce on.

Dad paid off the taxi at the Green and it drove off. Before he could put his wallet away I held out my hand. 'Shopping money, please.'

He fished out a twenty-pound note and handed it over. 'Pick up a bottle of their excellent Chianti, will you?'

I shook my head. 'If you want wine you'll have to come in the deli with me.'

'Whatever for?' Dad thinks shopping's beneath him.

'Regulations concerning the purchase of alcoholic drinks,' I said. 'I'm too young to buy booze, remember?'

Dad's got very little idea about the law of the land. Either that or he doesn't think it applies to him. He sniffed disdainfully and we headed for the deli.

Once inside, Dad selected a bottle of Chianti and handed it to the pretty Italian girl behind the counter. He paid for it and she put it in a plastic bag and handed it back with his change. He handed the bag to me.

'You see to the rest, Matthew. I'll be over by the fountain.'

He stalked out of the shop.

I asked for some freshly-made pasta and a carton of hot clam sauce.

The Italian girl gave me her usual dazzling smile and I wondered for the hundredth time if it meant she fancied me. One day I was going to summon up enough nerve to find out. Bottling out as usual, I paid and left.

As I came out of the shop I nearly bumped into a small man who had suddenly appeared in the doorway. He had a brown, wrinkled face and a shock of white hair and he was wrapped in a many-coloured blanket. He was a picturesque-looking figure, but you get all sorts on the Green.

'Sorry,' I said and started to move round him.

Then he spoke. '*Señor* Matthew, there is danger, great danger.'

I stared down at him. His brown eyes seemed bottomless. There was something hypnotic about their burning gaze. 'Sorry?' I said foolishly.

He pointed. 'See!'

Two men were talking on the other side of the road. The one with his back to me wore a long black raincoat. The man facing me was short and stocky, with olive skin and a heavy black moustache. He was staring up at the tall man as if hypnotised. I saw something pass between them – something that gleamed.

The man in black turned away and I caught a glimpse of his face. It wasn't a face at all, but an horrific, distorted mask.

I looked again at the stocky man. He was holding a huge gleaming knife, staring at it with horrified fascination.

Suddenly he turned and dashed across the road towards Dad, who was standing at the fountain with his back turned, studying the stonework.

The stocky man hurtled towards him, the knife held high . . .

Chapter Three

MASK OF THE DEMON

'Dad!' I yelled. 'Look out!'

The traffic must have drowned my voice. He didn't turn.

I dashed through a gap in the oncoming cars, heading for the central island and the fountain. Even as I ran, I realised I wasn't going to make it in time. I felt the weight of my plastic shopping bags bumping at my side, glanced down and saw the projecting neck of the Chianti bottle.

I grabbed it, dropped the bags and hurled the Chianti bottle at the man with the knife . . . and missed. It's not easy to throw accurately while you're running.

Curving up in a trajectory that was far too high, the spinning bottle struck the stonework of the fountain just above Dad's head. The results were spectacular. The bottle burst, showering Dad with

Chianti and broken glass. Still, it got his attention all right. He spun round with a roar of rage.

Distracted, the stocky man turned too – and saw me pelting towards him. Not for long though. The sight of the big gleaming knife in his hand brought me skidding to a halt. For a second we stood staring at each other – and suddenly I saw a sort of red glare flare up in his eyes. With a scream of rage, he switched targets and threw himself at me.

At the same moment Dad wiped the Chianti from his eyes and saw what was happening. He launched himself at the attacker in a heroic rugby tackle, missing by centimetres as the stocky man took off after me.

Some time ago I'd read a book on self-defence and one particular piece of advice had stuck in my mind. If attacked by someone with a gun or a knife, the book had said, at a time when you yourself are unarmed, carry out step one in the self-defence programme: run like hell!

There were various other steps you could take if you wanted to be more heroic and disarm your opponent, but step one was good enough for me.

I turned and ran, the stocky man at my heels. I crossed the road and set off along the edge of the

Green, my pursuer pounding behind me. The Green is roughly triangular in shape and it's pretty large. When I reached the edge, I instinctively turned, crossed the road and ran along the next leg of the triangle. I wanted to stay near Dad in an area where there were people about. I certainly didn't want my attacker to catch up with me in some empty side-street.

With the knifeman at my heels, I did a complete circuit of the Green in record time.

Glancing quickly round, I saw Dad on the ground by the foot of the fountain, surrounded by concerned passers-by and struggling to get up.

As I completed the circuit, I realised that my pursuer was catching up. My own fault, I suppose. Free of school and compulsory games, I'd let my standard of fitness slip. Too many Cokes and ice creams.

The stocky man however seemed tireless, buoyed up by some superhuman energy. I glanced over my shoulder and saw that he was still gaining on me, knife held high and face distorted with hatred.

Vowing to join the Hampstead Harriers if I ever got out of this alive, I desperately tried to speed up. Behind me the heavy footsteps pounded ever closer.

Suddenly I heard what I'd been hoping for – the screaming of a police siren and the sound of a car drawing up behind me. Somebody somewhere must have dialled 999.

I turned, panting, and saw the police car pull into the kerb just ahead of my pursuer. Three policemen jumped out, drawing their truncheons.

Warily they closed in on the man with the knife.

It was all over very quickly.

As the stocky man slashed at the nearest police-man, the one on his left raised his truncheon. It looked dangerously short – until, with a flick of his wrist, he extended it to a long baton and brought it sweeping down. It struck the knife, smashing it from the stocky man's hand. My attacker disappeared under a pile of blue-uniformed bodies.

I hurried across to the fountain where Dad was still trying to get up, hampered by the concerned little group around him.

'You must lie still and wait for the ambulance,' a large, bossy lady was saying. 'You've lost a great deal of blood!'

'It's not blood, it's wine, you silly woman,' shouted Dad. 'I'm perfectly all right, I tell you!'

'Concussed, poor fellow,' someone muttered.

I pushed my way through the little crowd and

looked down at Dad. It was no wonder they were all so concerned. With his white shirt and much of his grey suit soaked in Chianti, he looked like the victim in an exceptionally gory slasher movie.

'It's all right, everyone!' I shouted. 'It really is wine, not blood.' I reached down and helped him to his feet. 'All right, Dad?'

'Just about. You?'

'Fine, just a bit puffed. The police arrived and sorted things out.'

Dad looked ruefully down at his ruined clothes. 'You might have chosen some less spectacular way to warn me.'

'I was trying to clobber the bloke with the knife,' I said. 'Your wine shower was just an unfortunate side-effect!'

A uniformed police sergeant shoved his way through the crowd and stopped, aghast, at the sight of Dad. 'Better lie down, sir, the ambulance is on its way.'

'Then you can cancel it,' snapped Dad. 'My son threw a bottle of red wine at our assailant. He missed, the bottle broke and most of the wine went over me.'

With an effort, the police sergeant recovered his cool. 'I'm glad to hear you're not hurt, sir. In that case, I must ask you to come down to the station and give us a statement.'

Dad opened his mouth to protest, but I got in before him. 'We'll be right with you, Sergeant,' I said. 'I just need to make a quick phone call.'

I headed for one of the little cluster of phone booths by the fountain.

Some time later we were still down at the police station and things weren't going at all well.

Not surprisingly, the police were puzzled and suspicious about what had happened. They seemed to find Dad's story – that he'd never seen the stocky man before and had no idea why he'd been attacked – rather hard to take.

By now we were in an interview room being questioned by a tough-looking detective sergeant. His manner was abrupt and he was a bit short on tact. Dad didn't take to him at all. The detective sergeant's none-too-subtle hints that Dad might be involved in the drugs trade went down particularly badly.

Not surprisingly, Dad blew his top. 'For the last time, Sergeant, I have no idea why this happened. No doubt the poor fellow is one of those unfortunates released into the community too soon.'

'On the contrary, sir, the man is a perfectly respectable Spanish waiter with no criminal record and no history of mental trouble.'

'Then why don't you ask him why he attacked me?'

'Naturally we've tried, sir,' said the detective sergeant through gritted teeth.

'And what does he say?'

'He said the demon made him do it. That's all we could get out of him. Apart from that he seems perfectly sane, though he's badly shaken up.' He paused for a moment. 'Then there's this business of the unusual weapon,' he went on. He pointed to the knife, which lay between us on the table in a plastic evidence-bag. He consulted a piece of paper. 'It's an Inca sacrificial knife, stolen from the British Museum just a few hours ago. Some kind of ceremonial mask was stolen at the same time. Would you know anything about that, sir?'

'Why the devil should I?' snapped Dad. 'Ask your Spanish waiter. Perhaps he's some kind of religious maniac. He stole the knife and the mask and picked me out at random for a sacrifice.' He rose, looking as dignified as he could in his Chianti-soaked suit. 'I should like to leave now, Sergeant. I'm leaving the country first thing tomorrow and

I have a great deal to do this evening.'

'I must insist that you remain and help us with our enquiries,' said the detective sergeant menacingly. 'And you can forget all about leaving the country until this matter is cleared up.'

The phone on the table rang and the detective sergeant snatched it up. 'Yes? What? All right, show him in.' He turned to Dad, a triumphant gleam in his eye. 'A detective inspector from Special Branch has turned up,' he said. 'He says he knows all about you! Now maybe we'll learn what's going on.'

A few minutes later a young constable opened the door and showed in a large, fair-haired young man in a serious, dark suit.

Dad stared at him in astonishment then turned to me. He opened his mouth to speak, I gave a quick shake of my head and he shut it again. We'd both seen the large young man before. In fact, we knew him well. It was Jim Wainwright, Ms Alexander's assistant.

'This is chummy here, Detective Inspector,' said the detective sergeant, nodding towards Dad. 'He's been chucking his weight about, but I knew he was too good to be true. Know him, do you? What is it? Drugs? Terrorism?'

Ignoring him, Wainwright turned to Dad. 'Sorry

about this, sir, I got here as soon as I could. Soon have you out of here.' He swung round on the astonished detective sergeant. 'I do indeed know this man, Detective Sergeant. He is Professor James Stirling and he and his son Matthew leave the country tomorrow on a Government mission of vital importance. If he is hindered or delayed in any way, there will be repercussions at the highest level. You can turn them over to me now, I'll take full responsibility.'

The detective sergeant raised objections. Jim Wainwright crushed them and, minutes later, we were ushered out.

A black Bentley saloon was parked right outside the police station, guarded by a uniformed constable. There was a chauffeur at the wheel. The constable saluted. Jim and Dad and I got in the back and we glided away.

'Well done, Jim,' I said. 'You're not really an inspector in the Special Branch, are you?'

'I've got a warrant-card that says I am. Mind you, I've got another card that says I'm a gas inspector!' He glanced quickly at Dad. 'I like a glass of wine myself, Professor, but isn't this over-doing it?'

'Keep your jokes to yourself, young man,'

snapped Dad. 'This suit was ruined on Government service and I shall expect your department to replace it.'

Jim Wainwright grinned. He was used to Dad. 'I'm sure the secret funds can stand it, sir.' His voice became serious. 'My orders are to stay with you tonight and get you to the airport in the morning. We've got men guarding your flat, they'll be there all night.'

I had a sudden attack of the shivers as we made the short drive to our block of flats. Delayed reaction, I suppose. I looked at Dad but he was just looking grumpy, dabbing at his wine-soaked suit with a handkerchief. It didn't seem to have sunk in yet that someone had tried to kill us. I hadn't really taken it in properly myself. It was a comfort having Jim Wainwright to look after us, but I was still pretty uneasy.

Within hours of our accepting the mission, our unknown enemies had tracked us down and tried to kill us – here in England, close to where we lived! What kind of dangers were waiting for us in Peru?

Chapter Four

THE VISION

It took the Spanish conquistadors months of hard sailing to reach Peru. It's a bit quicker these days – but it's still quite a journey. It takes around twenty hours by air, depending on the route and on stopovers. There's no direct route from the UK. We were flying by way of America, with a stopover in Miami.

People grumble about long-haul flights, but personally I quite enjoy them. I even like airline food. Mind you, since we were on a Government mission and had diplomatic status, we were flying first class, which always helps. Comfortable, reclining seats with lots of leg-room, frequently-arriving trolleys loaded with free food and drinks . . . There were video and audio channels and there was even a power-point for my laptop.

As usual, Dad ate everything put in front of him,

gave the free champagne a good hammering and eventually drifted off to sleep, snoring rhythmically.

Back at the flat on the previous evening we'd sent out for a Chinese meal – my pasta had got lost in all the confusion. After the meal we'd spent some time discussing recent events with Jim, though without really getting very far. Clearly, our enemies had found out about our mission to Peru and taken steps to get rid of us before we even got started.

'What baffles me is how they found out so quickly,' said Jim. 'I mean, this was all top secret. Except for the minister, nobody knew except me, the boss and Colonel Santera.'

'Ministers have been known to leak information,' said Dad sourly.

'Not this one,' said Jim definitely. 'He's used to dealing with intelligence matters, he'd make a clam look chatty.' He paused. 'I don't know much about Colonel Santera but the boss seems to think highly of him.'

'So do we,' I said.

'I quite agree,' said Dad. 'Of course these Latin American types do tend to be rather excitable but Santera is a professional.'

'The British Museum robbery didn't produce

36

any clues,' said Jim. 'Our only lead seems to be this Spanish waiter. We're checking up on him now but there's nothing yet. Still, there's got to be a connection and a pretty strong one.'

'Not necessarily,' I said.

Jim looked surprised. 'Come off it, Matt, if he's willing to kill for them, he must be a member of their organisation. That or a freelance killer. If we can find out who runs him, or who hired him . . .'

'I think he was just a casual passer-by,' I said. 'The man in black made him do it. After all, he gave him the knife.'

I'd told Dad and Jim, and the police, about the man in black. For some reason I hadn't mentioned the old Indian who'd warned me.

'The man with the mask?' said Dad. 'But surely he must have known him already?'

'Perhaps not,' I said. 'Didn't Carlos say something about a sacred mask with mystic powers?'

Jim stared at me. 'Are you saying this character with a mask can go up to anyone and turn him into a killer?' He shook his head. 'I've dealt with plenty of terrorists in my time. But someone who can pick his assassins off the street . . .' He paused awkwardly. 'Ms Alexander knows what happened. She says if you want to change your minds . . .'

'I was given to understand this was a mission of international importance,' snapped Dad. 'I don't intend to be deterred by some stray lunatic. It's quite possible the whole thing was simply an unfortunate coincidence.'

We'd got on with our packing and gone off for an early night after that. Jim was spending the night on the sofa.

In bed, I found my mind was churning over too much for sleep. I got up, logged on to the Internet and looked up everything I could find on the Incas and on Peru. There was masses of material, far too much to take in that night. I downloaded everything that seemed in the least relevant and went back to bed.

Next morning, Jim had driven us to Heathrow. He'd used his security pass to see us right on to the plane. 'We weren't able to get anyone on the plane with you,' he said. 'The flight was fully booked with VIPs – we had to bump a couple of minor diplomats to get you two on. But you'll be met in Miami – we've contacted the American security services. They'll send someone to see you safely on to the next leg of the flight. Colonel Santera will meet you in Lima.' He grinned. 'At least we can get you there alive. After that, it's up to you. Good luck!'

The journey went on – and on and on. Dad woke up, took in more food and drink, and went back to sleep again. In the final few hours, I got bored with watching movies and listening to old comedy routines on audio and decided it was time to catch up on my research.

Now, in the peace and quiet of the plane – peaceful, that is, except for the low drone of the engines and the louder drone of Dad's snoring – I studied the files. When I'm going into a new and dangerous situation, I like to be well prepared.

A few hours later I switched off the laptop and leaned back, my head spinning. My mind was full of golden temples, gorgeously robed priests and blood-drenched human sacrifices.

It was an amazing story. In fact, it was two amazing stories.

The Incas had started out as a small tribe, centred around their capital of Cuzco high in the mountains of Peru. They were just one among many tribes, all constantly at war with their neighbours.

Then something happened. The Incas suddenly became conquerors, sweeping all before them. Their empire grew with amazing speed. At its height it stretched from Colombia to Chile, covering 984,000 square kilometres. Then Pizarro arrived and conquered the Inca empire in two years – *with two hundred men!* Oh, they had horses and guns and armour and swords made of better steel. But all the same – two hundred men.

There were thirty thousand men in the army of the Inca king when he first encountered Pizarro, and many more troops in the interior. The Incas should have won with ease. It might have cost them hundreds, perhaps thousands, of lives but they had soldiers to spare, battle-hardened veterans ready to die for their leader. Surely they could have swarmed all over the invading Spaniards?

But – they hadn't. It was as if their spirit had been defeated, as if they had lost the will to fight.

The Incas had had extraordinary victories, followed by an even more extraordinary defeat. Why? What had caused it?

I drifted off to sleep.

I was standing on a hilltop, watching two armies clashing in battle. They fought with swords, spears and clubs. Soon one army gained the upper hand, driving their enemies back.

They were led by a tall, gorgeously robed man with

a golden sun orb on his breast. Somehow I knew that this was Atahuallpa, the Inca king.

He urged his men forward, his eyes glowing red with the lust of battle . . .

The scene changed and I was standing in a city square, its borders lined with armed men. Swarthy, bearded, hard-faced men wearing breastplates and steel helmets, carrying swords and pikes and muskets. They were dirty and ragged and starved-looking, but their weapons and their armour were clean and bright. They were Spaniards – conquistadors.

There was a wooden stake in the centre of the square, faggots of wood piled round its base.

A door in an impressive temple-like building opened and guards led out their prisoner.

It was Atahuallpa, the Inca king. His head was bowed in defeat and the golden sun orb was gone from his breast. A black-robed Spanish priest walked by his side, reading from the open Bible in his hands.

A tall man with a long beard stood a little aside from the others. He looked much like the other con-quistadors but his air of command marked him out as their leader, Francisco Pizarro.

The soldiers led the king to the stake and bound him to it. At a nod from the tall man, one of the soldiers produced a leather thong, stepped behind the king and swiftly and efficiently strangled him.

Soldiers put torches to the faggots and soon the king's dead body was engulfed in flames.

The bearded man looked on impassively. The flames seemed to reflect a red glow into his eyes.

The scene changed again . . .

I stood on the edge of a jungle in which stood a stone Inca shrine.

From somewhere within the shrine came a fiery red glow. Two men stood before the shrine. One was an old Indian, his hair white, his brown face wrinkled and lined. The other was a taller, more impressive figure, in the gorgeous golden robes of an Inca high priest.

Both men were chanting, sometimes separately, sometimes together.

The glow from the shrine flared higher. The chanting became louder . . . Slowly the red glow faded and died away. The two men turned and moved away into the jungle, going their separate ways.

I turned and saw, without surprise, a small white-haired figure, wrapped in a colourful blanket, standing beside me. He looked up and smiled. 'You see, Señor Matthew?' he said. 'First Victory, then Defeat, then the Binding. It is all perfectly clear, is it not?'

And just for a moment it was.

The vision faded . . .

. . . and I was back in my seat on the plane being offered a drink by a well-meaning air-hostess.

I sipped a Coke and tried to recapture my dream or vision or whatever it was.

'First Victory, then Defeat, then the Binding.'

Somehow I knew that those few words held the answer to our problem. The only trouble was, I hadn't the slightest idea what they meant . . .

Some time later, Dad woke up with a grunt, blinked and looked at his watch. 'Wake up, Matthew,' he said, as if I was the one who'd been asleep. 'We'll soon be arriving in Miami.'

Not long after that we did. Or rather in Miami airport, which is just like any other airport only busier, noisier, larger and more confusing.

As we reached the bottom of the exit ramp, a tall figure with crew-cut, fair hair and horn-rimmed glasses stepped forward. 'Professor Stirling? Matt?'

I stared suspiciously at him for a moment and then grinned. 'Chuck! How are you?' I turned to Dad. 'You remember Chuck Roberts? He was with us last time we were in Miami. That Bermuda Triangle business.'

'Yes, of course,' said Dad, who'd clearly forgotten all about him.

Chuck Roberts was a junior agent in an American security agency. The last time we'd been in Miami, his boss, Mr Simmonds, had assigned him to work with us.

'Mr Simmonds sends his regards,' said Chuck. 'He'd've come himself but there's this conference on so he sent me, since at least I know what you look like.'

'Nice to see you again,' I said. I liked Chuck, there was a sort of puppy-like enthusiasm about him.

Chuck pointed to a vehicle parked a little way away, two tough-looking men standing beside it.

'It's a heck of a way to your next departure gate,' he said. 'I checked the route myself earlier. So I commandeered this.'

'This' was a little buggy with two wide rows of seats. The seats were back-to-back, one lot facing forwards, one backwards. The sort of thing you got to ride on when you were too infirm, or too important, to walk.

'VIP transport,' said Chuck proudly. 'Your baggage is transferred automatically but this will save your legs. A couple of airport security people just volunteered to act as escort.'

Dad and I got on the backward-facing row of seats and Chuck sat on the forward-facing one. One of the security men got on beside him and the other one got into the driver's seat. Lights flashed, a siren sounded, and we moved away, under the envious eyes of other passengers starting their long hike.

We sped across vast and busy concourses, past shops and bars and restaurants and then along endless corridors.

Suddenly a familiar voice whispered, '*Señor* Matthew, take care! These men are not to be trusted.'

There was nobody close by – but a small, white-haired Indian was walking away down the corridor.

I was about to warn Chuck when things were taken out of my hands. Chuck said, 'Hey, the driver's taken a wrong turn, I checked this route.'

'Short cut,' said the security guard beside him.

After a moment Chuck said, 'Short cut, hell!' and leaned across to the driver. 'Turn this thing round, you're going the wrong way.'

I turned to see what was going on, just as the security guard beside Chuck produced a heavy automatic pistol and pointed it at him. 'Shuddup and siddown,' he said calmly. 'Or I'll blow your heads off, right here and now.'

Chapter Five

DEATH IN LIMA

It was the confidence in his voice that got up my nose. The sheer arrogance. As if all he needed to do was wave a gun at us and we'd cower down and do as we were told.

Chuck suddenly yelled, 'Jump him, Matt, I'll get the driver!' I didn't think twice. I jumped up, took a flying leap over the back of the seat and hurled myself at him. My knees hit him in the chest, sending us both off the side of the moving buggy. We hit the smooth floor of the corridor together, rolling over and over.

We crashed into the wall and the guard broke free, the gun still in his hand. We both scrambled to our feet and he aimed the gun at my head, clearly intending to carry out his threat. I leaped on him again, grabbing his gun arm with both hands and desperately shoving his arm upwards.

The gun went off with an incredibly loud noise and the bullet smashed one of the lights set into the ceiling. Immediately alarms started ringing and I heard the sound of distant shouts and pounding footsteps.

The guard turned to run and I rugby-tackled him, bringing him to the ground. As he started to get up I hung on to his legs, bringing him down again.

I regretted my impulsive move as soon as he hit the floor again. My opponent was bigger and stronger than I was – and he was the one with the gun. We wrestled furiously but I knew it was only a matter of time before he broke free and started shooting.

Dad came running over and hurled himself into the fray. He's a skinny old bird but he's stronger than he looks and he's always ready to have a go.

Between us we wrestled the gunman to the ground. Dad grabbed his ears and banged his head hard on the ground. The man went limp.

Gasping, Dad got up and helped me to my feet. 'Are you all right?'

As my anger died down I realised I was bruised here and there but not seriously hurt. 'I'm OK. More frightened than hurt.'

Immediately his concern turned to anger. 'That

was an incredibly rash thing to do, Matthew. You might have been killed.'

There's gratitude for you!

'We might all have been killed,' I pointed out. 'What do you think those characters intended to do when we got to wherever they were taking us?'

I turned back to the buggy which had come to a halt just down the corridor. Chuck had the driver in a painful-looking armlock and had relieved him of his gun. Reminded, I bent over the unconscious guard and took the gun from his limp hand.

A posse of very large American policemen came pounding down the corridor, all armed to the teeth. Covering me with his revolver the first policeman to arrive screamed, 'You! Drop the gun! Drop it now! Face down on the ground!'

I stared at him in amazement, then realised I still had the gun in my hand. They take guns very seriously in airports.

Handing his captive to the nearest policeman, Chuck came over and flashed his security pass. 'It's OK, officer, he's one of the good guys.' He pointed to the semi-conscious thug who was starting to stir. 'This is the one you want.'

I handed the automatic to the policeman. 'Here, you'd better have this.'

'Would someone kindly tell me what the hell's going on here?' he bellowed.

'Kidnapping and attempted murder, that's what,' snapped Dad. 'It's a disgrace. You people still haven't outgrown the Wild West! You're just not civilised.'

'Is that so?' said the policeman menacingly. 'Now listen, Limey –'

Time for another of my diplomatic interventions. 'Let's leave the explanations to Chuck, shall we, Dad?' I said hurriedly.

Chuck took the policeman aside and began talking in a low, urgent voice. More policemen hauled the thug to his feet and our attackers were led away. And that was pretty much it, really.

Like policemen everywhere, the American cops wanted us to come down to the station, answer lots of questions and make a statement. Rising to the occasion, Chuck flourished his secret agent credentials again and insisted we be allowed to catch our plane. He won in the end but it all took time.

When we were finally given permission to go on our way, Chuck looked at his watch and gave a yell of alarm. 'We'll only just make it! Come on, you guys, if I don't get you on that plane old man Simmonds will murder me!'

Chuck jumped behind the wheel of the buggy and we got on behind him. It only took him a moment to work out the simple controls. He swung the buggy in a wide U-turn and we rocketed off to the departure gate, lights flashing and siren screaming.

A tense female voice was coming from the loudspeaker system. 'Will Professor James Stirling and Matthew Stirling, passengers in transit for Lima, *please* report to Gate 18. This is their final call.'

So much for security, I thought. Now the whole airport knows who we are and where we're going.

Still, if recent events were anything to go by, everyone knew already.

We piled off the buggy and Chuck produced his security pass and ushered us on to the plane.

I grabbed his arm. 'Chuck, listen, see what you can find out about those gunmen, will you? Who they work for, who hired them. Send the information to Colonel Santera in Lima; your department will know where to reach him.'

Chuck promised to do his best, said a hurried goodbye and backed away. A disapproving stewardess showed us to our seats. We walked along the aisle, running the gauntlet of irate glares from our fellow passengers. No doubt they thought we'd been whooping it up in one of the airport bars.

We'd been amongst the first passengers to board the plane at Heathrow, so there'd been little opportunity to observe the passengers boarding behind us. This time we were last, not first, and as we approached our seats I saw someone I recognised. A very tall man with white hair and a neat white beard. It took me a moment to place him. It was Don Ramon, the man we'd met, or rather Carlos had met, in the foyer of the Savoy Hotel. He looked at me in surprise and I realised I must have been staring at him. His companion, a sharp-faced man with a thin moustache, gave me an angry scowl. No doubt they were all cross with us for delaying their plane.

I turned away hurriedly and followed Dad to our seats and we began the second leg of our journey.

Lima is the capital of Peru, a big, bustling, sprawling city. In a sense, all big cities are much the same. You get traffic – and traffic jams – air pollution, a variety of museums, hotels large and small, cafés, bars and nightclubs, shopping districts and business districts complete with glass skyscrapers.

Lima has all this and more. It has prosperous suburbs for the well-off, and sprawling shanty towns around its edges for the very poor. It has decaying, but still impressive, Spanish colonial mansions and large and splendid civic squares complete with flower-beds, fountains and statues. It also has a warm, dry climate, although it can be blanketed in mist and fog from April onwards. Luckily it was only March, so we touched down at Lima's Jorge Chavez airport in brilliant sunshine.

Carlos was there to meet us. Once again his appearance had undergone a change. He wore a creased white suit, a garish tie and a battered straw hat. There was dark stubble on his chin. He was even carrying a cardboard sign with STIRLING crudely scrawled on it. He looked every inch the slightly seedy tourist guide.

He led us to a bright blue and badly dented Chevrolet. As we got in I caught a glimpse of Don Ramon and his entourage getting into an impressive-looking official limousine.

Carlos got behind the wheel of the Chevrolet and drove us the seven kilometres into town. I'm inclined to think that journey was our most dangerous experience so far. The driving in Lima has to be seen to be believed. The roads were crowded with suicidal drivers in every kind of vehicle from jeeps to limousines. Big American saloons seemed to be the most popular. I soon understood why the Chevrolet, like so many of the cars around us, was covered with dents.

On the way we brought Carlos up to date with recent events – the attack in London and the second attack in Miami.

'Someone is very anxious that you should not reach Peru,' he said. 'But they have failed and you are here. Now that you are in Lima I shall take steps to keep you safe. I have already arranged for there to be security people in your hotel.'

The Gran Hotel Bolivar was on the corner of the Plaza San Martin. It was a massive place, very old and very luxurious, with an air of faded splendour.

Hordes of hotel staff descended on us and carried away our luggage. Carlos led us inside and we stood looking in amazement at the vast, ornate foyer. Carlos smiled at our reaction. 'This was once the finest hotel in all Lima,' he said. 'Now it is a little behind the times. Nevertheless, the Gran Hotel Bolivar has character! Also, there is live music on Saturday nights!'

'I shall look forward to it,' said Dad solemnly.

Carlos grinned and handed us over to the hotel staff, saying he would call for us next day after breakfast when we'd recovered from our journey.

He advised us to stay in the hotel until then. 'Lima is not the safest of cities, especially at night,' he explained in an undertone. 'I suggest you dine in the hotel. This area, like the hotel, has gone down a little since the old days.'

Next day Carlos met us in the foyer as promised.

'Welcome, distinguished *señores*,' he said loudly in his tour-guide voice. 'I have come to take you on a walking-tour of our glorious city of Lima.'

He led us out on to the sunlit plaza and we followed him through the teeming colourful streets. We ended up in the imposing Plaza Mayor in the heart of the city. The central fountain was crowned with a statue of the Angel of Fame.

'Actually it's a reproduction,' said Carlos, sticking to his role of guide. 'Apparently the original angel flew away in 1900!'

It was a warm and sunny morning and the square was crowded with people. Most wore the same casual jeans and T-shirt kind of clothing that I wore myself, though here and there you saw the traditional colourful blankets of the Indian.

Dad looked around the crowded scene with his usual complacent air of having seen it all before.

'All very picturesque but it's not what we're

here for, is it? When do we start work?'

'This morning,' said Carlos, lowering his voice. 'There is to be a special conference of the Crisis Committee – an assembly of all those concerned with the problem. It will take place at the National Security Agency. It is quite close to here. Meanwhile, this walking-tour helps to keep up your cover as innocent tourists.'

Suddenly we heard a commotion from a nearby street, getting louder. There were shots fired and some ragged figures appeared, running across the square, pursued by green-uniformed soldiers.

Carlos grabbed the nearest soldier and flashed a security pass. They had a brief conversation in Spanish and the soldier ran on.

'What happened?' asked Dad.

'Another riot,' said Carlos sadly. 'Three people killed. They ignored orders to disperse and three of them produced machetes and attacked soldiers who were armed with machine pistols. They seemed to think bullets could not harm them.' He sighed. 'The whole city is on the edge of revolt.'

'Then we'd better get to this meeting and see what can be done about it,' said Dad crisply.

Carlos nodded gloomily. I suddenly had the feeling he didn't have much hope.

Neither did I – but we had to try.

Dropping back into character, Carlos described some of the tourist attractions around us in a very loud voice. On one side of the square was Lima's enormous cathedral, painted a somewhat surprising shade of ochre. On the other, the ornate Government Palace, guarded by sentries in traditional blue and white uniforms.

'Over there is the Presidential Palace,' he said, indicating yet another large imposing building. 'The Conquistador Pizarro was assassinated there in 1541. His throat was slashed by the rapier of an assassin and he died in a pool of blood. It is said that as he lay dying he drew a cross in his blood and kissed it.'

Suddenly the dark, haunted face of the man in my dream came back to me. The leader of the conquistadors with the red glare in his eyes. So he too had come to a bad end, like his Inca victim . . .

I came out of my momentary daydream to hear Carlos still droning on about the local sights. Only half-listening, I noticed a familiar figure standing on the corner nearby. An old, white-haired Indian wrapped in a blanket. The man I'd seen back in London, outside the Italian deli on the Green and again in Miami airport. He raised a finger and pointed warningly at a young Indian moving straight towards us. He too was wrapped in a colourful blanket and he carried strings of beads and native ornaments. He looked harmless enough, but all the same . . .

I interrupted Carlos's lecture and indicated the young Indian. 'I think we're about to be on the receiving end of a local sales drive,' I said.

Carlos looked where I was pointing and sighed. 'One of the *ambulantes*,' he said. 'Street peddlers. The police try to drive them from the city centre but they always return. I will chase him away.'

He waved his arms and shouted something in Spanish at the *ambulante*.

The man continued to move closer, smiling ingratiatingly and waving his strings of beads.

Carlos shouted again, more angrily this time.

Still ignoring him, the *ambulante* kept coming – and took a gleaming machete from beneath his blanket.

He had a curiously blank expression, as though drugged or hypnotised. And something flickered in his eyes: a kind of red glare . . .

Chapter Six

THE *QUIPU*

Carlos reacted to the approaching danger with amazing speed.

As soon as the machete appeared, his hand flashed beneath his coat, reappearing with a huge automatic pistol.

He shouted something urgent in Spanish – clearly an order to stop. The *ambulante* ignored him.

He shouted again and fired a warning shot over the man's head. The boom of the shot was astonishingly loud. Heads turned all over the square and startled birds wheeled into the air.

The *ambulante* screamed a kind of high-pitched chant. Then he rushed towards us, machete raised.

Carlos fired twice, two shots in rapid succession. The *ambulante* crumpled and fell. Nothing dramatic – he didn't go flying backwards like people do in Westerns. He just dropped. He was so close that the fringe of his coloured blanket touched Carlos's shoes.

I looked up at Carlos and saw that he was scanning every centimetre of the square, alert for fresh danger. I looked at him, stunned. This wasn't the humble, helpful Carlos of Easter Island or the seedy Lima tourist guide or even the polished Latin charmer of the Savoy Hotel. This was a trained, efficient killer.

It struck me that nobody in the crowded square was showing much interest in what was happening. On the contrary, they were all moving purposefully away. They don't hang around gunfights in South America. People know better.

I noticed a handful of dark-suited men detaching themselves from the departing crowd and hurrying towards us. I touched Carlos's arm in warning.

He looked at the approaching men and smiled grimly. The gun disappeared inside his jacket and suddenly he was the old Carlos again.

'It is all right, Matthew,' he said. 'They are friends. Not very useful friends, it appears, but friends all the same.' He looked down at the crumpled body and I saw, to my astonishment, that his eyes were full of tears.

'*Pobrecito*,' he murmured. He crossed himself. 'It is a terrible thing to kill a man, Matthew.'

Dad, who'd been stunned into silence until now, was starting to recover. Like me he was shaken and scared. As often happens with Dad, it came out as anger.

He glared accusingly at Carlos. 'You shot that man down in cold blood!'

'What choice did I have?' asked Carlos sadly.

'Be fair, Dad,' I said. 'If it wasn't for Carlos he would have carved us up with that machete.'

'He could have wounded him, given him a chance to surrender.'

Carlos gave a scornful laugh. 'Just like in the movies, you mean? Bang! The weapon flies from the killer's hands, leaving him subdued, clutching his lightly-grazed wrist! No, Professor, not in the real world. If someone comes to kill you at close range, you shoot for the heart. The heart and, if you have the time and the skill, the head. That way you are sure – and alive.'

Dad got a grip on himself. 'I'm sorry, Carlos,' he said stiffly. 'No doubt you know your own business best, though it's not a business I care for.

Nevertheless, I must thank you for saving both our lives.'

Carlos bowed his head, accepting both apology and acknowledgement.

The dark-suited men were surrounding us by now and there was a sudden babble of excited Spanish. Carlos snapped out an order and they all shut up. He gave them a withering glance.

'These gentlemen are agents of the Peruvian intelligence service, temporarily under my command. Their job was to surround us with an invisible security screen.' He sighed. 'Naturally they ignored the *ambulante*. To be honest, so did I at first. After all, everyone knows *ambulantes* are no more than a harmless nuisance.' Carlos glanced at his watch. 'We shall be late for our conference.'

He snapped out more orders and we moved away.

Two of the security men stayed with the body, presumably to deal with the regular police when they arrived. Even in South America, a dead man in the street means a few legal formalities. I saw one of the men kneel down and start searching the body. I shuddered and looked away. After a moment, I started to shiver and feel sick. Three attempts to kill us in three days!

The other three men moved along with us in a loose semicircle, keeping much closer this time. Carlos was taking no more chances.

A thought struck me as we walked through the busy, sunny streets.

'What did that man shout, just after you fired the warning shot?' I asked.

Carlos thought for a moment. 'He said, "We do not fear you, your bullets cannot harm us." '

'I thought so,' said Dad, reminding us that he spoke Spanish. 'And that tells us something. Something very significant.' He was getting over the shock now and was almost back to his old superior self.

'Like what?' I asked.

'It confirms that this – movement, or whatever it is, has some kind of religious or supernatural basis.'

'How do you work that out?' I asked.

I had a pretty good idea, actually, but I thought it might cheer him up if I gave him a chance to lecture us a bit.

'Oh, it's a common pattern,' said Dad loftily. 'The illusion of invulnerability – you remember Carlos spoke of it earlier. You find it in African tribes, in the *moro* rebels in the Philippines.

There's some kind of secret society involved as a rule. They hold a ceremony before battle and the high priest gives the warriors some kind of magic potion. He tells them it will make them immune to enemy bullets.'

I thought of the huddled body in the square.

'I gather the potion doesn't always work too well.'

'It does in a way,' said Dad thoughtfully. 'The potion usually contains some powerful hallucinatory drug. Under its influence the warriors *believe* they're immune to bullets, which makes them incredibly hard to kill. They can suffer terrible wounds and still go on fighting. During the rebellion in the Philippines, the American marines had to change their official automatic pistols over to the big .45 calibre models. No smaller bullet could stop a charging *moro* guerrilla.'

Dad's just full of these fascinating facts.

Carlos led us to another, quieter square with a neglected-looking statue of a conquistador on horseback in the centre.

'Pizarro again,' he said. 'Not such a popular figure in Lima these days. There was even a movement to have the statue taken down but it came to nothing.'

Just off the square there was an old-fashioned,

discreetly anonymous office building, its roof festooned with elaborate communication aerials. Carlos led us into the foyer and showed a pass to an armed guard.

An ornately decorated lift carried us up to another, more impressive, marble foyer with a set of double doors on the far side. Beyond the doors was a huge old-fashioned conference room with a vast gleaming mahogany conference table stretching down the centre.

The walls of the conference room were lined with portraits of distinguished-looking gentlemen in nineteenth century dress, all with stern expressions and impressive moustaches. Gathered round the table were their twentieth century equivalents. Some wore beautifully cut suits, others were in uniform. Some of the uniforms were sober and workmanlike, others were gorgeous, with epaulettes and gold braid.

Politicians, soldiers and policemen, I thought. A few senior ministers and high-ranking officers to add dignity to the proceedings and those of lower rank who'd be doing the actual work.

All the seats round the big conference table were filled, except for three at one end. They were for us.

Carlos showed us to the seats and we sat down.

Every head turned towards us. Carlos remained standing and made a brief speech in Spanish, presumably apologising for our lateness and introducing us to the distinguished company. Then he too sat down.

An important-looking old codger with a white moustache rose at the other end of the table and made a long speech. He sat down and someone else rose.

So it went on. Speech after speech. Some seemed long and boring, some angry and passionate. I could only go by the tone, but I guessed that arguments and counter-arguments were being offered. A big wall-map of Peru was pulled down and one of the soldiers rose and spoke briefly, indicating various areas with a pointer.

Eventually even Dad had had enough. He rose suddenly and barked, '*Señores!*'

Everyone looked at him.

He made a short and snappy speech in fluent Spanish, bowed, pushed back his chair and strode from the room. Carlos and I followed.

In the foyer outside, he turned appealingly to Carlos. 'Lunch, please, Carlos!'

'I am glad to see you have not lost your sense of priorities, Professor,' said Carlos gravely.

'What did you say, Dad?' I asked as we went down in the lift.

'I said that honoured as I was to be consulted, I could not possibly give an opinion till I had absorbed and considered all the available information. I promised to report back as soon as possible and begged them to excuse me.' He turned to Carlos. 'I hope I didn't seem rude?'

'On the contrary, you impressed them greatly,' said Carlos. 'Such arrogance can only belong to true genius!'

Carlos's security team were waiting in the entrance foyer. As we came out of the lift, they were joined by the two men he'd left in the square. Presumably the body had been taken away by now.

One of the two men hurried over to Carlos, spoke briefly and handed him something in a plastic evidence-bag. Carlos nodded and shoved the bag in his pocket. He snapped an order at the man behind the reception desk and minutes later two cars appeared outside the main door.

We got into one, the security team piled into the other and we drove away.

We had lunch at an expensive-looking restaurant called *Las Brujas de Cachiche* on the *Avenida Bolognesi*.

'It is one of the finest restaurants in Lima,' said Carlos as we were ushered to our table. 'Even the name is interesting. It means The Witches of Cachiche. He explained that Cachiche was a small town nearby, famous for its witches and healers.

At Carlos's recommendation we had a traditional Peruvian seafood dish called *ceviche*, a spicy mixture of fish, shrimp, scallops and squid, with corn, sweet potatoes and onions. Dad and Carlos shared a bottle of Peru's finest white wine. I had a slightly weird, but not unpleasant, gold-coloured drink called Inca Cola, the locally produced Coke.

His good temper restored by food, drink and ferociously strong black coffee, Dad sat back with a sigh of relief.

'I'm sorry to walk out like that, Carlos, but I just couldn't bear any more of that – that talking shop!'

'The Crisis Committee is far too large,' agreed Carlos. 'Everybody of influence with any interest in the affair insisted on having a place on it. They wrangle endlessly and take no effective action. They will go on talking for the rest of the day.'

'I believe you,' said Dad. 'If you'll get me transcripts of all relevant information, intelligence reports, that kind of thing, I'll study them and see if I can find a place to start.'

'You shall have them today,' promised Carlos. He put a hand in his pocket and pulled out the plastic bag. 'This was found on the dead Indian.'

He emptied the bag on to the table. It held a short length of twisted rope from which hung a tangle of different-coloured knotted strings.

Dad peered at it. 'What is it, some kind of charm?'

Carlos shook his head. 'It's a *quipu*,' he said. 'The Inca never developed a written script. Instead they used these. They could send messages, keep accounts, record their history – all with these.'

'It could be important,' I said. 'Maybe it'll give us some clue to who's behind all this.'

'I fear not,' said Carlos.

'Why not?' I persisted. 'Surely it must have been important to the man who carried it?'

'Perhaps so,' said Carlos. 'Unfortunately, the secret of the *quipu* has been lost for hundreds of years. There is nobody alive who knows how to translate it!'

Chapter Seven

SUSPICION

We sat for a moment, gazing in sheer frustration at the useless clue. Then something struck me – a flaw in Carlos's logic.

'Hang on a minute,' I said. 'Somebody must be able to read this thing.'

Dad raised an eyebrow. 'Who?'

'The man who was carrying it for a start. Why carry a message you can't read?'

'The man who was carrying it is no longer in a position to help us,' said Dad acidly. 'Besides, he may have been carrying the thing just as a symbol, a lucky charm.'

'Maybe, but I doubt it,' I said. 'These people want to bring back the good old days of the Incas, right? This *quipu* is exactly the sort of thing they'd use to send secret messages. An unbreakable code, loaded with historical symbolism.'

'You may well be right, Matthew. But it doesn't take us much further. We don't know the other people in the conspiracy – and they'd scarcely be likely to help us if we did!'

'All the same,' I said obstinately, 'it means that the knowledge *has* survived. There must be someone who can translate for us.'

'Perhaps there is,' said Carlos.

'Who?' demanded Dad.

'My cousin, Don Ramon!' said Carlos triumphantly. 'You saw him briefly in London, remember? If anyone can translate this thing, he can.'

Carlos put the *quipu* back in its plastic bag, summoned a waiter and asked for the bill and a telephone.

Minutes later, we were on our way.

Don Ramon held the *quipu* up to the light, studying it with rapt attention. 'Extraordinary!' he breathed. 'A modern *quipu*!' He looked up at us. 'All the surviving *quipu* are naturally hundreds of years old but this one might have been made yesterday. I thought the art of making them was lost.'

'What about the art of reading them?' I asked.

We were in Don Ramon's stately colonial

mansion, just off the Plaza Mayor. It was the home of the Institute of Inca Studies and also his personal residence.

A black-clad man with sharp features and a thin black moustache had opened the door to us. He looked vaguely familiar and I remembered seeing him on the plane with Don Ramon. He showed us into the study, a book-lined room with heavy, old-fashioned furniture. It might have been the study of some Victorian manor house – except for the slowly revolving ceiling fan and the exotic plants outside the open French windows.

Don Ramon had risen from behind his old-fashioned desk, embraced Carlos, and greeted Dad and me with gentle, old-fashioned courtesy. He had a quality of warmth and charm about him that made you like him immediately. I suppose it is what is called charisma.

There was a pause for polite small talk and the serving of sherry, brought in on a silver tray by the sharp-faced man. Don Ramon introduced him as, '*Señor* Miguel Aguero, my invaluable personal secretary and confidential aide.' Aguero bowed stiffly, served the sherry and withdrew.

The formalities over, Carlos had produced the *quipu* and explained our problem.

Now Don Ramon turned the *quipu* over in his hands, running long thin fingers along its threads.

'I have studied the *quipu* for many years,' he said. 'I know a little, a very little of its secrets.'

'Can you translate for us, Don Ramon?' asked Dad.

'In detail, no,' said Don Ramon calmly. 'Not without a great deal of further study. However, perhaps I can give you some hint of the general meaning.'

'Please do,' said Carlos. 'Anything you can tell us, however little, will be of the greatest help.'

We watched with breathless anticipation as Don Ramon stood, eyes closed, running the *quipu* through his fingers again and again.

'Some important event is about to take place very soon,' he said at last. 'A rally, a meeting, a ceremony, I cannot be sure.'

'Does it say when this event is to take place?' asked Carlos eagerly. 'Or where?'

Don Ramon shook his head. 'That I cannot tell. If you could give me more time, I could consult my reference books.' He waved an arm around the book-lined room. 'The answer may well lie in one of these volumes.'

'Of course,' said Carlos. 'I am sorry to impose

on you, Don Ramon, but the matter is urgent.'

'We need the precise location, date and time,' said Dad bluntly. 'Without it the information is of very little use.'

'I shall do my best for you,' said Don Ramon gravely. 'Call me later this evening and I may have news for you.'

We said our goodbyes, leaving the *quipu* with Don Ramon.

The sharp-faced man led us back to the front door. As he walked ahead of us down the long corridor, it struck me once again that he looked familiar. I'd seen him on the plane, of course. But there was something else . . .

Carlos and his team escorted us back to our hotel, where a security man was waiting with a bundle of documents and dossiers. We carted them up to our suite, ordered drinks from room service and held a quick conference. The security team stayed outside, lurking in the foyer and in the corridor outside our suite.

Dad looked ruefully at the bundle of reports. 'I'll do my best to work my way through these, but I doubt if they'll tell me anything new.'

'Can I assist in any way?' asked Carlos. 'If not, I have much to do.'

Dad shook his head. 'There's no point in you sitting round and watching me read. I suggest you join us later and we'll plan our next move – if there is one.'

Carlos nodded. 'Very well. Before I return I will call Don Ramon in case he has any more news for us.' He finished his drink and rose to leave. 'I shall leave a security team in place. From now on you will be guarded at all times.'

After Carlos had gone, Dad looked at me over his glasses.

'Let me tell you my plan, Matthew.'

'Don't bother,' I said. 'I can guess. You want us to go home.'

'Precisely! We can do no good here, we should never have come. We've survived three assassination attempts. I don't want to risk a fourth.'

'So what are you going to do?'

'I propose to skim through these reports and make a note of any useful observations. Then I shall pass my notes on to Carlos and ask him to book us seats on the next flight home.'

I shook my head. 'I think that would be a mistake.'

'Don't be ridiculous, Matthew,' snapped Dad. 'After three attempts to kill us, it simply isn't safe to stay.'

'I don't think it's safe to go, either,' I said. 'Not till we've sorted things out here. I very much doubt if we'd reach home alive. Here we've at least got the protection of Carlos and his security team.' I paused. 'For what it's worth . . .'

Dad frowned. 'What are you getting at?'

'It's bad enough having some unknown enemy trying to stop you before you get started,' I said. 'What's really scary is when that enemy seems to know exactly where you're going to be all the time!'

'You mean, there's been a security leak?'

'What do you think? We have lunch at the Savoy, make a quick visit to Ms Alexander's HQ, and by the time we get home someone's got an assassination attempt all lined up. We catch a plane and they're waiting for us at the Miami stopover. Here in Lima, we're ambushed on the way to a top-secret conference.'

'Only Ms Alexander and Carlos knew of our plans,' said Dad.

I nodded. 'And, in Lima, only Carlos.'

There was a moment of silence. Then Dad said, 'Carlos? That's impossible. Besides, he brought us here.'

'He was forced to bring us here,' I pointed out.

'At the request of the Peruvian Government. Carlos has Indian blood, remember, and he's sympathetic to the Indian cause. Suppose he's part of this conspiracy? Suppose he gets stuck with the job of investigating it – and gets landed with us as well? Suppose he's afraid we might find out too much?'

Dad shook his head. 'I still can't believe Carlos is our enemy. It's too fantastic. Just this morning he saved both our lives. Why would he do that if he's on their side?'

'Maybe they mounted the attack without telling him,' I suggested. 'He could have reacted instinctively. And we were surrounded by his security team. It would have looked bad if he'd stood back and let us be killed.'

Dad thought hard for a moment. 'Everything you say is perfectly possible in theory, Matthew, but I still can't bring myself to believe it.'

'Neither can I, really,' I said miserably. 'But if there's no other possibility –' I broke off as a piece of the jigsaw suddenly dropped into place.

'What is it?' asked Dad.

'Just a sort of vague idea.'

'What?'

'It's too vague to talk about yet,' I said. 'I need some time to think it through.'

'What about Carlos?'

'If I'm right, Carlos will be back here shortly. Back with important news.'

Dad gave an exasperated sigh and got on with his paperwork. Since the documents were all in Spanish there was no way I could help. I mooched around the suite for a bit, still brooding, then wandered out on to our little balcony and looked down at the crowded, sunlit square.

The small figure of an old, white-haired Indian stood looking up at me. For a moment our eyes met, then he vanished into the crowd.

I went back into the room, scooped up my laptop and went into the bedroom. Sitting down at the small corner table, I switched on and accessed the files on Inca history I'd downloaded in London.

Remembering my dream on the plane, I looked up the account of the death of Atahuallpa, the last great Inca king.

Pizarro had lured him into an ambush and then arrested him. He had extracted a huge ransom in gold and then executed him anyway. Before his execution, Pizarro had given Atahuallpa a choice. He could convert to Christianity and be mercifully strangled or retain his Inca beliefs and be burned alive . . .

Shuddering at the gruesome story, I remembered the end of my dream, the high priest and the little shaman chanting at the jungle shrine.

First Victory, then Defeat, then the Binding . . .

The Incas had enjoyed incredible success then sudden shattering defeat at the hands of an inferior force.

Pizarro had enjoyed the same success for a time – and then his good fortune had faded away and he'd died miserably at the sword of an assassin.

Success and failure, success and failure. Success changing from one side to the other – *and then back again?*

Somehow that was the key to it all.

Switching off the laptop, I wandered back into the sitting-room. Dad was still ploughing dutifully through the reports.

A pile of photographs lay on the side of his table and as I walked by they slid over the edge for no apparent reason, scattering over the carpet. I bent down and gathered them up, leafing idly through them and putting them back on the pile.

They showed a variety of Peruvian types, some Indian, some Hispanic.

'What's this all about?' I asked.

'It's a kind of rogues' gallery,' said Dad. 'People

they think might possibly be involved in the conspiracy. None of them means anything to me, of course.'

I stared down in astonishment at the photograph in my hand. It showed a small, white-haired old Indian, wrapped in a faded blanket.

The one who had warned me in London, in Miami, and again here in Lima. The one I had seen in my dream and who had been standing in the square below a moment ago.

I turned over the photograph and saw a hand-written note in Spanish.

I passed it to Dad. 'Who's this one?'

Dad glanced at the note. 'He's a famous shaman called El Viejo – the old one. He's supposed to have tremendous powers. They say he's hundreds of years old. They don't know if he's involved in the conspiracy or not. Whenever they try to pick him up for questioning, he just disappears . . .'

The door was suddenly flung open and Carlos burst into the room.

'Great news! Don Ramon has deciphered more of the *quipu*. He now knows the place where the event will take place. It is Machu Picchu. Do you know it? It is a lost city of the Incas – the ruins of a city – in the jungle not far from here.'

'Does he know when this event happens?' I asked.

'Or exactly where?' asked Dad. 'As I remember, Machu Picchu is a very large site.'

'Not yet. But even that he hopes to discover soon.' Carlos was in a state of high excitement. 'Meanwhile we must go to Machu Picchu to investigate further.' He looked eagerly from one to the other of us, a little hurt that we didn't share his enthusiasm. 'I think we should leave at once,' he went on. 'Who knows how soon this mysterious event will take place? If we can capture the ringleaders . . . I have arranged for transport and accommodation.'

Dad gave me a worried look, remembering our earlier conversation.

'Matthew, what do you think we should do?'

I studied the photograph of El Viejo for a moment, as if his wrinkled old face held the answer. Were we moving towards a solution, or walking into a trap?

There was only one way to find out.

'Carlos is quite right, Dad,' I said. 'We must go to Machu Picchu.'

Chapter Eight

THE LOST CITY

Surrounded by jungle, the ruins of Machu Picchu, lost city of the Incas, lie high in the Andes between two great peaks.

There are three ways to get there. You can walk, trekking along the Inca trail, a route popular with the legions of backpackers who come every year. It takes three to five days. You can go by train, riding for hours through some of the most spectacular mountain scenery in the world. Or, if you're in a hurry as we were, you can go by helicopter.

Helicopter travel is quick but it's far from comfortable. The noise is shattering and the vibration rattles your bones. The view through the transparent dome made it all worth while.

It was an incredible flight between towering mountain peaks, their slopes covered with forest and jungle, their summits crowned with snow.

Machu Picchu itself is an amazing sight. On an intricately terraced spur of land between the mountains lies a complex network of broken granite walls. Some of them rise almost to roof-height, others are much lower. Seen from the air it resembles a giant maze, threaded by winding paths. Here and there the maze is broken up by patches of open grassland.

We touched down on the helipad in Machu Picchu Pueblo, the little town close to the ruined city, where a self-drive car was waiting. There were just the three of us now. The little civilian helicopter had been too small to bring Carlos's security team. They were to follow us as soon as they could get here.

Carlos drove us to the predictably-named Hotel Machu Picchu, a surprisingly posh place for such a remote spot. I said as much to Carlos.

'You forget the tourists, Matthew,' he said. 'Many thousands come to Machu Picchu every year. There are dozens of hotels, everything from cheap boarding houses to top class hotels such as this.'

We checked into our rooms – even Dad admitted they were sufficiently luxurious – and met for dinner in the hotel restaurant. After an excellent meal, with more Peruvian specialities, we discussed our next move.

'Don Ramon says he is near to a breakthrough with the *quipu*,' said Carlos. 'I have given him the number of this hotel, and he will call if he has news.'

As if on cue, a waiter came saying there was a call for Carlos. He left the table for just a few minutes and returned fizzing with excitement.

'That was Don Ramon. He has cracked the code of the *quipu* – broken it completely! He says it relates to a special ceremony to be held, here at Machu Picchu, tonight, at moonrise. He has given me the precise location. Only the leader, the re-born Atahuallpa, will be there, with his high priest. We can capture them both!' Carlos produced a map of Machu Picchu and spread it out on the table. 'The ceremony is to be held here, at the Sacred Stone, just beneath the North Terrace.' He looked at his watch. 'We can easily reach the nearest entrance before moonrise.'

'Hang on a minute,' protested Dad. 'Shouldn't we wait until your security people arrive? Suppose there are more people at this ceremony than we bargain for?'

'Don Ramon was insistent that there would be only two. If we wait for the security men we may be too late. We cannot miss this opportunity.' Carlos paused. 'Or, rather, I cannot miss it. If you both wish to wait here for my security team, I shall quite understand.'

I could see that Dad was torn between his very reasonable doubts and his fear of being thought chicken.

I myself had no doubts. I knew that I had to go.

'Something tells me we ought to go with Carlos, Dad,' I said. 'I want to be in at the end of this thing. And we may still be able to help.' I looked hard at him. 'Please, trust me.'

After a moment he said, 'Very well, Matthew. I defer to your instinct, it has served us well before. We'll come with you, Carlos.'

Dusk was falling as we came out of the hotel. Carlos drove us along winding mountain roads until we came at last to a gate with a low, modern building beyond.

'The warden's lodge,' he explained. 'Officially the ruins close at five p.m. I have made special arrangements for us to be admitted.'

It seemed odd to think of a sacred lost city with a five o'clock closing-time but that's the tourist industry for you.

We got out of the car and a shadowy figure emerged from the lodge and opened the gate for us.

We went inside and he closed the gate behind us.

Carlos led us into the ruins of the lost city.

It felt strange and eerie, following the winding paths between the jagged stone walls. As we walked, a full moon began rising in the stormy sky above us and there was the occasional rumble of thunder.

'We must hurry,' whispered Carlos.

He led us steadily onwards, pausing to consult the map by the light of the moon.

The path began climbing steadily upwards and soon both Dad and I were gasping for breath.

'It is the altitude,' said Carlos. 'You have not yet had time to get used to it. Take deep breaths.'

We staggered on. The journey seemed endless but we came at last to a massive flat-topped rock in a little clearing at the very edge of the ruins. Close behind the clearing the mountainside rose sharply upwards.

We stopped, studying the dark bulk of the Sacred Stone. Were we too soon? I wondered. Or too late?

The Sacred Stone began to glow with hellish red light. The red glare revealed two figures standing with their backs to us, facing the rock. One was very tall and thin, the other equally thin but smaller. Both were gorgeously robed.

Carlos gave a sigh of satisfaction and drew his automatic pistol. Raising it, he stepped forward.

'Stop! You are both under arrest.'

The figures turned. With a gasp of horror I saw that the faces of both were terrifying, demonic masks.

Even Carlos took an involuntary step backwards. Recovering himself he ordered, 'Remove the masks.'

Both figures obeyed.

The very tall man was Don Ramon. The smaller was Miguel Aguero, his personal secretary and confidential aide.

Carlos was gazing at his cousin with unbelieving horror.

'Don Ramon!'

'No longer,' said the tall, robed figure. 'I am Atahuallpa, King of the Inca. It is my destiny to restore our empire to its former glory. The work has already begun. You will hinder it no longer.'

Ignoring this, Carlos said, 'My regrets, Don Ramon, but I must still do my duty. You are under arrest.'

Don Ramon's eyes glowed red and the big automatic pistol flew from Carlos's hand. He moved to go after it but seemed frozen to the spot.

I felt myself held by the same invisible force. I glanced at Dad and saw he too was motionless.

'Hold on, Dad,' I whispered. 'Help is at hand, I can feel it.' I didn't mean Carlos's security men either. Somehow I knew that something was coming. Something else.

The robed figures replaced their demon masks and Aguero produced a ceremonial knife from beneath his robes.

'Mount the Sacred Stone and prepare to die,' ordered Don Ramon. 'Your heart, and the hearts of your companions, will be sacrifices to our future glory.'

Slowly, unwillingly, Carlos took a few dragging steps forward. The Sacred Stone glowed a brighter red until it was almost transparent. Inside, I saw the shape of a twisted alien form.

Carlos put his foot on the lowest of the rough steps carved into the side of the Sacred Stone, as a jagged streak of lightning cracked across the night sky, followed by a tremendous crash of thunder.

Someone stepped into the clearing.

It wasn't an impressively terrifying form, like the robed, demon-masked figures in front of the Stone. It was a small, white-haired, brown-faced Indian, wrapped in a faded blanket.

It was El Viejo, the shaman.

He began chanting in some ancient tongue – presumably the old Inca language. Immediately the red glow from the Sacred Stone faded a little and we found we were free of its grip.

Carlos ran back towards us and began searching the undergrowth at our feet for his automatic pistol.

'Don't bother, Carlos,' I said. 'This isn't a matter for guns any more.'

He still continued looking though, and I didn't blame him.

El Viejo went on chanting. I could feel the alien force inside the Sacred Stone battling the power of his words.

The demon-masked figures began chanting in opposition. The red glow from the Sacred Stone flared brighter and then dimmed, flared brighter and dimmed, in a supernatural battle of wills. The hideous alien shape inside the stone writhed angrily.

Suddenly I felt something reaching out to me from El Viejo, a kind of appeal.

Concentrating fiercely, I joined the whole force of my will to his, throwing all my mental strength into the battle.

For a moment the Sacred Stone flared a brighter

red. The alien figure inside twisted as if in agony, then exploded in a burst of brilliant red fire.

The Sacred Stone went black.

There was a brilliant flash of lightning, an ear-splitting crack of thunder and a sudden downpour of tropical rain. We heard a strange, rumbling, slithering sound.

'Quick!' shouted Carlos. 'The mountain is falling!'

We turned and ran.

At what seemed like a safe distance we turned and looked back. A whole section of mountainside was breaking away. We looked on in horror as it rumbled down in a mixture of mud and rocks, completely obliterating the Sacred Stone and the masked, robed figures before it.

I turned and saw El Viejo gazing at me across the clearing.

'The Spell of Annihilation is complete,' said a voice inside my head. *'The Demon is destroyed at last. I thank you for your help. I fear I grow old. I needed a young, strong mind to strengthen my own.'*

I stared back at him, unable to reply.

The old man smiled. *'I see you are still confused,* Señor *Matthew. Permit me to explain.'*

Chapter Nine

THE FAREWELL

'It had to be Don Ramon,' I said. 'There was no one else – except you, Carlos, and neither of us could really bring ourselves to believe that!'

We were back in the hotel, having changed into dry clothes, and were sitting with drinks of hot chocolate before a blazing fire in the lounge. I was doing my best to explain the inexplicable to Dad and Carlos, both shaken by recent experiences. I should have been more shaken up myself but the afterglow of my link with El Viejo left me strangely calm.

I explained the importance of the assassination attempt in London.

'It meant there had been an *immediate* leak,' I said. 'Of information possessed only by you, Carlos, and Ms Alexander. I couldn't believe it was her – but I couldn't believe it was you either, not really.

Then it struck me. Who was the one person you *might* have talked to? Someone you had known all your life, always looked up to and respected as a great man?'

Carlos bowed his head. 'It is true. When we met in London I asked his advice. I told him everything. I can never forgive myself.'

Dad and I made consoling noises, and I went on with my story.

'I suspect Carlos did such a good sales job on us that he convinced Don Ramon we were dangerous. Remember, Don Ramon wasn't expecting to have to attack anyone in London. The magical equipment he needed was all back here in Lima. He just had time to send his sidekick Aguero to the British Museum to steal the Inca demon mask and the sacrificial knife. Ramon invested the mask with supernatural power, and Aguero whizzed to Hampstead and hypnotised that unfortunate waiter into trying to kill us.'

'What about the attempt in Miami?' asked Dad.

'Don Ramon must have been behind that too. He was a wealthy man and he had probably spent some time in Miami.'

Carlos snapped his fingers. 'There was a report from your friend Chuck, back in Miami. He said your two attackers are professional hit-men. They work mostly for the Mafia, but sometimes they freelance.'

'There you are, then,' I said. 'Either Don Ramon or Aguero must have had contacts with the Mafia. They knew what plane we were on and they just arranged a straight commercial hit. He could have fixed it up by phone from London when Aguero told him the first attempt had failed. Once we were in Lima, a third attempt was simple.' I paused. 'The trouble is, Don Ramon took me in too. Lots of pennies didn't drop till it was almost too late.'

Dad raised an eyebrow. 'Such as?'

'Such as the way he didn't ask more questions when we brought him the *quipu*. Then there was my recognising Aguero. I knew his face from the plane, but somehow he looked familiar from the back, when he led us down that corridor. It wasn't till much later I realised. I'd seen him walking away on the Green, just before the first attack.'

'I suppose that business about translating the *quipu* message was all a fake?' asked Dad.

I nodded. 'I doubt if there ever was a message. The thing was probably just a symbol, as you suggested. Don Ramon simply invented a message to lure us into a trap.'

I took a swig of my hot chocolate. 'I think that's about it. With Don Ramon gone, the heart will go out of the rebellion.'

But I wasn't getting off so easily.

'Oh no you don't!' said Dad. 'Where did Don Ramon get these powers he used? What really happened at the Sacred Stone tonight? How does it all tie in to Inca history?'

'I can only tell you the story I was told,' I said slowly. 'I can't justify it or explain it; you'll have to take it or leave it.'

'Fair enough, Matthew,' said Dad. 'Go on.'

'All right. The story is that hundreds of years ago some alien entity came to Peru. It had great psychic powers, and it chose to interfere in human affairs. It boosted the powers of the Inca kings. That's why their empire rose so rapidly.'

'So why did it fall so easily to the conquistadors?' asked Carlos.

'Because the alien changed sides.'

'Why?' demanded Dad. 'Why would it do that?'

I shrugged. 'Perhaps for amusement. Perhaps it saw in the conquistadors human pawns more ruthless than the Incas. Whatever the reason, it changed sides. The Incas lost their fighting spirit, the handful of conquistadors became all-powerful.'

'So what happened next?' asked Carlos.

'An Indian shaman realised what had happened. He allied himself with an Inca high priest and they found a way to cast out the alien and imprison it inside the Sacred Stone. The conquistadors lost their supernatural edge but by then it was too late, the Incas had lost the battle and the conquistadors held on to their power.'

'How did Don Ramon become involved?' asked Carlos.

'He loved the Incas and studied them all his life. Somehow he must have come across the story of the alien and discovered a way to free it. Once free, the alien changed sides again. I think it just liked the idea of stirring up a bloody revolution. I think it was basically evil and exulted in cruelty and destruction.'

'And now it is destroyed?'

I nodded. 'For good, I hope.'

Carlos sighed. 'How am I to put all this in my official report?'

'Leave out the supernatural side altogether,' I advised. 'You tell your Crisis Committee that you trapped and eliminated the leaders of the conspiracy. They won't ask too many questions.'

Carlos sighed. 'I hate the thought of Don

Ramon's guilt becoming public knowledge.'

'No reason why it should. Don Ramon was tragically killed by a mudslide while excavating at Machu Picchu.'

'And the old Indian?' asked Dad.

'A descendant of the shaman who originally bound the alien.'

That or the original, I thought, though I didn't say so.

'Once the alien was free, it was safe inside the Sacred Stone,' I went on. 'He had to persuade it to expose itself so he could destroy it. That's what happened tonight.'

Next day we flew back to Lima and Dad and Carlos made their report to the Crisis Committee. Carlos gave Dad and me credit for great if mysterious services. Dad made a sizzling farewell speech, telling the committee they'd got off lightly this time and if they didn't treat the Indians better they could still be in for a lot more trouble.

We said goodbye to Carlos, who had a lot to do mopping up the remains of the revolution, and caught the next plane home.

As we climbed up the gangway Dad said, 'All that business about alien entities and shamans –

just a fable, you know. Pure folk-myth. It was all South American politics really.'

'Of course it was,' I said soothingly.

Dad's very good sometimes at ignoring the evidence of his eyes.

As we entered the plane there was the usual line-up of cabin staff, welcoming us on board.

The first in line was an elegant young man, the second a motherly-looking woman. The third was an old, white-haired Indian with a wrinkled, nut-brown face, wrapped in a faded blanket.

'Goodbye, *Señor* Matthew, goodbye, *Señor* Professor,' he said. 'Have a pleasant flight.' We shook hands and his hand was warm and dry.

He shook hands with Dad too and we moved on towards our seats.

When I looked back he wasn't there.

Looking a little dazed, Dad slumped into his seat.

'Don't worry, Dad,' I said. 'Look at it this way – you've just shaken hands with a folk-myth!'